Stories from Abergelli Street

Nicola Davies

Illustrated by
Elaine Franks

With thanks to staff and pupils
at Llangors school for their help

First Impression—2002
Second Impression—2004

ISBN 1 84323 075 5

This volume is published with the support of the
Arts Council of Wales.

Printed in Wales at
Gomer Press, Llandysul, Ceredigion SA44 4QL

Contents

Introduction

If you go to Bethesda bus station at ten o'clock on a Wednesday morning, you'll be just in time to catch the number 3 and a bit bus. If you sit by the window, you'll see the river shining below as you cross over the bridge.

The bus will swing out of the town and wind round the hills as if it's climbing a helter-skelter. At the top of the highest hill, you'll look down past the forest to the buttercup field where Brinley Baseball scans the sky and wishes he could fly like a bird.

Down below, just past the buttercup field, are the slate roofs of Abergelli Street. Cleo lives here with her dog, Mr Kidwelly. Just down the road, you'll see Mr and Mrs Rhossili and the five pigeons, Deri, Dai, Dylan, Digri and Twp. The end house has beds of brightly coloured flowers and a greenhouse. That's where Councillor Pedr Pizza lives and grows his prize leeks.

The bus twists and turns on its way to Abergelli Street. Hang on tightly as we shoot downwards round the narrow bends and tight corners.

Abergelli Street . . . here we come!

Caradog Among the Pigeons

Autumn leaves, soggy as damp cornflakes, were falling onto Abergelli Street. They stuck to Mrs Rhossili's broom as she swept the path. They clogged up the rake when she tackled the lawn.

'Sweep up here next,' said the five pigeons. 'Leaves are plastered all over our roof.'

'If it's your roof, you can do it yourselves,' said Mrs Rhossili and she went indoors to put on the kettle.

It was cold up on the roof. The pigeons strutted back and forth on the wet slates and pushed damp leaves onto the path. Then they flew down to see Mrs Rhossili. 'We're going to build ourselves a warm nest on the roof,' they said. 'What can we make it from?'

Mrs Rhossili liked the pigeons. They were always peeping in at the windows and telling her all the gossip. 'Help yourselves to some twigs,' she said, 'and I'll find something soft to line your nest.'

The pigeons collected twigs and branches and wove them together. Mrs Rhossili gave them some balls of fluffy wool, orange and green to line their nest. They helped themselves to some

pairs of stripy socks from the washing-line and Mr Rhossili's best cap. 'We'll keep our eggs in the cap,' they said.

When Mr Rhossili came home from the barber's, he was furious.

'That nest is a mess,' he told his wife. 'If you don't remove it, I will. And are those my socks sticking out of it?'

As soon as Mr Rhossili went out again, the pigeons flew in.

'Where has Mr Silly gone?' asked Dai, Deri and Dylan.

'His name's not Mr Silly,' said Mrs Rhossili. 'And he's gone to buy a cap. He's lost his.'

'Oh, he has, has he?' said the pigeons.

'I don't suppose you've taken it, have you?' asked Mrs Rhossili.

'Us?' said the pigeons, innocently. Then they flew off to play their favourite game . . . Sliding Down the Rooftops.

Next morning, when Mr Rhossili went out, the pigeons flew into the kitchen again. Mrs Rhossili was standing on a stool, changing a light bulb.

'What are you doing up there?' the pigeons

asked. 'Get down, Mrs Rhossili. Up in the air is our bit of the room.'

They waited until she had replaced the bulb, then flew round her head, asking questions non-stop. 'Where's Rhossili gone?' asked Dylan. 'Are you coming to admire our nest?' asked Digri. 'Why is your tongue sticking out?' asked Twp.

Mrs Rhossili ignored the pigeons. She got a large mixing-bowl out of her cookery cupboard and poured in flour, sliced in butter and threw in brown sugar. Then she stirred it all with a big wooden spoon.

'Are you making something good to eat?' asked the pigeons.

'I'm baking a cake,' said Mrs Rhossili.

'Good,' said the pigeons. 'Is it our nest-warming cake?'

Mrs Rhossili grated a large bar of chocolate into the cake.

'She's making us a chocolate cake,' the pigeons told each other.

'No, I am not,' she said. 'This cake is for Mr Rhossili.'

'Tell him to make his own cakes,' said the pigeons.

Mrs Rhossili broke two large eggs into a bowl

and beat them until they turned into a deep yellow goo. She poured the goo into a bowl.

'Are those our eggs?' asked Dai. 'Don't put them into Rhossili's cake.'

'You haven't laid any eggs!' said Mrs Rhossili. 'These are hen's eggs.' She stirred the goo into the cake mixture. Then she poured the mixture into a round tin and put it into the hot oven.

'She's going to feed our cake to Mr Silly,' said the pigeons. They were so cross, they dropped feathers all over his favourite chair.

Mrs Rhossili took a cup of tea into the garden. She had a faraway look on her face. Soon, the pigeons came to disturb her.

'Where's that Rhossili gone?' asked Dai, Digri and Twp.

'To collect newspapers,' said Mrs Rhossili, sipping her tea.

'That Mr Silly gets sillier and sillier,' said Dylan. 'Why is he always collecting newspapers?'

'It's his secret,' said Mrs Rhossili. 'After he's collected them, he's going to buy a long-handled broom.'

'A broom?' said the pigeons. 'Why does he want a broom?'

Mrs Rhossili finished her tea and walked up the path to admire her roses. The pigeons followed her.

'Tell us why he needs a broom,' insisted Dai.

'He means to sweep your nest off the roof,' said Mrs Rhossili.

'What a cheek,' squawked all the pigeons. 'He can't do that to our lovely nest. You must stop him, Mrs Rhossili.'

'He won't listen,' she said. 'Perhaps he'll listen when his stomach's full of chocolate cake.'

The pigeons were so upset they flew in and out of their nest, tidying it, then messing it up again. Then they sat on Mr Rhossili's photograph and dropped things on it.

While Mrs Rhossili was clearing up the droppings, the pigeons perched on her head and looked at her from upside down. 'Don't let him sweep our home away,' they said.

Mrs Rhossili had an idea. She went up to the spare bedroom. It was a big airy room with a large bay window. In front of the window, on the roof, was the pigeons' nest. Mrs Rhossili put fresh sheets and pillow-cases on the bed and dusted the dressing-table. Then she fetched a large piece of paper and some felt pens. She wrote a notice with blue felts:

She took the notice downstairs and stuck it onto the front window, for passers-by to see.

'Have you locked yourself out?' asked the pigeons. 'Shall we rescue you?' Then they saw the notice in the front window. They tried to read it, with difficulty.

'What's a REGDOL?' they asked. 'Can you eat it?'

'Of course not,' said Mrs Rhossili, turning the notice round. 'That's LODGER, not REGDOL. A lodger is coming to stay in the spare room.'

'Why?' asked Deri.

'To stop Mr Rhossili sweeping your nest away. If there's someone in the spare room, he won't be able to use his broom, will he?'

'Good idea,' said the pigeons. 'Aren't we clever to think of it?'

Mrs Rhossili took the chocolate cake out of the oven. It smelled wonderful. She put a cover over it, to stop the pigeons pecking it. Then she went up to the spare room, to make it ready for the lodger. She put a new duvet cover on the bed and was lining the drawers when the door-bell rang. 'Rhossili must have forgotten his key again,' she said.

But it wasn't Mr Rhossili on the front doorstep.

'Hello. I'm Caradog, your new lodger.'

'But you're a cat.'

'Yes, I am,' said Caradog, proudly. 'I am a cat and a lodger. I've brought my toothbrush, some soap and a face flannel . . . although I usually wash myself with my tongue. May I see my room now, please?'

Mrs Rhossili showed Caradog the spare room with the new duvet cover. 'Try the bed to see if it's comfortable,' she said. Caradog sat on the bed and bounced up and down to test it. Then he stretched out and pretended to go to sleep. 'Is that enough?' he asked. 'Have I tested it properly?'

'Is it comfortable for you?' asked Mrs Rhossili.

'Yes, thank you. Very.'

'How about the view?'

Caradog looked out of the window and saw the pigeons' nest. 'What is that?' he asked.

'That's the pigeons' nest.'

'Do pigeons wear caps and socks?' asked Caradog, surprised.

'Of course not,' said Mrs Rhossili. 'They just wear feathers and sing. In Welsh.'

'I like a bit of singing myself,' said Caradog.

'Would you like a cup of tea . . . or a saucer of milk?' asked Mrs Rhossili.

'Tea, please,' said Caradog, 'in a saucer.'

While they were having tea and biscuits, Caradog asked who else lived in the house.

'Just me and Rhossili,' said Mrs Rhossili. 'And the pigeons, of course. Deri, Dai, Dylan, Digri and Twp. Do you like pigeons?'

'Peaceful ones,' said Caradog. 'I'm on my holidays, you see, so I need peace and quiet.'

'You'd better meet the pigeons then,' said Mrs Rhossili, looking a little worried.

She opened the window and in flew the pigeons, talking all at once. 'Is this the lodger?' asked Dylan. 'What happened to its tail?' asked Twp. 'Why is it wearing spectacles?' asked Dai and Deri. 'Will it save us from Mr Rhossili and his broom?' they all asked.

'Would you like some of my biscuit crumbs?' asked Caradog. He broke a biscuit into pieces and fed it to them. They made him feed them six times more.

'Have you seen our nest?' asked the pigeons.

'It looks very comfortable,' said Caradog politely.

'It's just for us five,' said the pigeons, hurriedly. 'There's no room in it for lodgers. Now, are you going to save us?'

'Save you from what?'

'From Mr Rhossili. He wants to sweep our nest off the roof.'

'You need a flag with *Private Property* on it,' said Caradog.

The pigeons liked the sound of that. 'Make us a flag now,' they said. 'And afterwards we'll let you play Sliding Down the Roof with us.'

'Just let me fetch my case from the front doorstep,' said Caradog. 'Then I'll make the flag.'

'You've decided to stay, then?' said Mrs Rhossili. 'The rent is £27 a week . . . Alright? '

'You can charge more if you like,' said Caradog. 'I don't mind how much you charge, because I haven't any money anyway.'

Caradog made a big flag from one of his pillow slips. He wrote on it with his special poster pens:

Pigeon Palace
Private Property
Do not remove.

Then he climbed out of his bedroom window and stuck the flag onto the nest. The pigeons became very excited. 'That Rhossili won't sweep our nest away now,' they said. 'It's our private palace.'

They were so pleased, they slid up and down the roof with their feet in the air. Then they flew in and out of the chimney. There were feathers everywhere, falling like grey snow.

When Mr Rhossili arrived home, he took the long-handled broom out of the van and carried it upstairs into the spare bedroom. Caradog was sitting on the duvet cover, reading a newspaper.

'Who are you?' asked Mr Rhossili, startled.

'I'm Caradog, your lodger. Are you the chimney-sweep?'

'No, I'm Mr Rhossili. I'm going to sweep that nest off the roof.'

'You can't do that,' said Caradog. 'This is my room now. Please take your broom away. And shut the door quietly after you.'

Mr Rhossili went downstairs. 'There's a lodger up there,' he said.

'That's Caradog,' said Mrs Rhossili. 'He's having a holiday in the spare bedroom.'

'He won't let me take my broom in.'

'Never mind, 'said Mrs Rhossili. 'Have a slice of chocolate cake.'

That night, when Mr Rhossili was fast asleep, Mrs Rhossili crept downstairs to get the rest of the chocolate cake. She carried it upstairs to the spare bedroom and tiptoed onto the roof to join Caradog and the pigeons. She even played Sliding Down the Rooftops with them, although she wasn't very good at it. Then everyone ate chocolate cake and watched the flag fluttering above the pigeon nest.

The pigeons flew along the road, telling the other birds about their private palace and their flag. 'Our lodger, Caradog, made the flag for us,' they said proudly.

Caradog and Mrs Rhossili stared across the rooftops to where the moon made dark shadows on the hills.

'This is a lovely place for my holiday,' said Caradog, happily, licking chocolate crumbs off his paws.

The Lost Scarecrow

One Autumn morning, Cleo went to her bedroom window and looked out across the garden, where trees held out their empty branches and a wooden gate opened onto a stony lane. The lane wound its way up a rocky hill to the green slopes of the forest. To Cleo's surprise, it looked as if a scarecrow was growing among the trees.

'That's funny,' said Cleo. 'I wonder how a scarecrow got up there.' Then she went down for breakfast and forgot all about it.

In the afternoon, Cleo looked out across the garden to the green fringe of the forest. The scarecrow was still there. His arms were pointing left and right and a woodpecker was perched on top of his head.

'I wonder what he's doing there,' said Cleo. (She was talking about the scarecrow, not the woodpecker). Then she went out to throw a ball for Mr Kidwelly and forgot about the scarecrow all over again.

That night, when the moon turned silver to gold, Cleo looked out and saw the scarecrow standing straight and alone in the moonlight. 'He must be lonely up there in the dark,' she said to herself.

Cleo crept downstairs to wake Mr Kidwelly. He was asleep in his willow basket, floppy ears hanging over the sides.

'Wake up, Mr Kidwelly. *Dere 'mlaen.* Come along.'

Mr Kidwelly sat up on his haunches and yawned. Then he trotted over to his dinner-bowl. It was empty.

'It's too early for breakfast,' said Cleo.

Mr Kidwelly trotted over to his special toy box. He nudged the lid off with his nose. Then he began to drag all his toys out of their box.

'It's too early for games,' said Cleo. She put his toys back in the box.

Mr Kidwelly cocked his head to one side and looked at Cleo as if to say, 'No food, no toys. So why did you wake me up?' He looked at his comfy basket, his warm, cosy basket. He clambered back in and closed his eyes.

'Wake up,' said Cleo. 'We're going to visit the scarecrow.'

Mr Kidwelly opened one eye and grunted.

Cleo went to the cupboard for a tin of dog food. She forked some of it into Mr Kidwelly's dinner bowl. 'Wake up, Mr Kidwelly. Time for breakfast.' Then she went to his toybox and got out his stripy green rubber bone. 'Wake up Mr Kidwelly. Time for games.'

Mr Kidwelly clambered out of his basket and inspected his bowl. He ate the dog food and drank some water. Then he picked up his rubber bone and dropped it at Cleo's feet. She threw it for him to catch.

After they'd played the throwing game ten times, Cleo said 'Now can we go for our walk please, Mr Kidwelly?'

Mr Kidwelly barked loudly and looked at his lead hanging by the back door. Cleo had to stand on a stool to reach it. She unhooked the lead and jumped down. She fastened it to Mr Kidwelly's collar. He wagged his tail. Then she stood on tiptoe to unbolt the back door into the night sky. She looked up and saw how beautiful the stars were. Then Cleo looked at the high ridge where the scarecrow stood alone. 'Come along, Mr Kidwelly,' she said, pulling at his lead.

Mr Kidwelly had never been out at night. He looked up at the dark sky and sparkling stars, and yowled.

'Be quiet, Mr Kidwelly,' said Cleo. 'You'll wake up Mam and Dad. It's only night-time. The lights will be back on again soon.'

Mr Kidwelly followed Cleo to the top of the garden, then out through the wooden gate.

'Now we have to climb the lane,' said Cleo. 'Watch your step.'

Mr Kidwelly looked up at the stony lane and down to the warm kitchen where his basket was. He began to howl.

'Be quiet,' said Cleo. 'You'll wake all the children. Stop behaving like a puppy, Mr Kidwelly. We're just going to visit the scarecrow and then we'll go straight home. Alright?'

They climbed the winding path up the hill. Whenever Mr Kidwelly tried to run back home to his warm bed, Cleo pulled hard on his lead. At last, they reached the top of the high ridge, where the scarecrow stood among the trees.

'Hello,' said Cleo,

The scarecrow said nothing, because even though his eyes were open, he was fast asleep.

The scarecrow had been dreaming for a long time. He was dreaming of when he used to live on Gwilym Gooseberry's farm. He dreamt about the time he saved a field of corn from a band of marauding magpies. He dreamt about the time he kept an eye on Gwilym's black lambs as they leapt among the buttercups. He dreamt about bees humming in Gwilym Gooseberry's hives. He dreamt about the river flowing fiercely past Gwilym's farm on its way to the sea.

'Please wake up,' said Cleo. 'We've come to visit you.'

The scarecrow woke from his long dream and looked down at Cleo and Mr Kidwelly. 'Visitors? For me?'

'I'm Cleo. And this is Mr Kidwelly,' said Cleo. 'We came to see how you were.'

'I'm not so dusty, thank you,' said the scarecrow.

'We thought scarecrows lived on farms,' said Cleo. 'What are you doing in the forest?'

'I've lost my farm,' said the scarecrow. 'It was Gwilym Gooseberry's farm, really, and he sold it to a supermarket. Now, instead of the hum of bees, there's only the hum of traffic on the motorway. Instead of Gwilym's black lambs among the buttercups, black rubbish-bags line lamp-lit streets. Instead of the shining river flowing under the stone bridge, a river of sparkling cars winds over the motorway.' And the scarecrow gave a sigh. Mr Kidwelly joined in with a long yowl.

'What's your name?' asked Cleo.

'Gwilym called me Bwgan Brain,' said the scarecrow, 'but you can call me Bwgan.'

'Is there anything I can do for you, Bwgan?' asked Cleo.

'Could you untie my arms, do you think?' said Bwgan.

Cleo stood on Mr Kidwelly's strong back and untied the scarecrow's arms. She was good at shoelaces, too. The scarecrow waved his arms about and wiggled his fingers. '*Diolch*, Cleo. Thank you for freeing me.'

'Anything else?' asked Cleo.

'I could do with a woolly hat,' said Bwgan. 'It gets quite cold up here when the wind blows.'

'I'll bring you one next time I visit you,' said Cleo. 'Anything else?'

'Well,' said Bwgan, 'there is something else you can do . . . please find something for me to guard. You see, Gwilym Gooseberry made me for a purpose. I'm supposed to guard things. The field of corn is gone, so I can't guard that. The black lambs are gone, so I can't guard them. And, by the way, you shouldn't be out on your own at night.'

Then something strange happened. Bwgan suddenly started to laugh. Then he began to jump about all over the place. He danced and laughed and ran in and out of the trees. Mr Kidwelly looked at Bwgan dancing and joined in, jumping up and down on his huge paws. Cleo looked at them both and then she began to laugh and jump about in the tall wet grass, in the moonlight.

'Why are we jumping about?' she said, at last.

'Because I have found something to watch over,' said Bwgan.

'What is it?' asked Cleo.

'It's you,' said the scarecrow. 'I shall watch over you and Mr Kidwelly. I shall begin by walking you both back home.'

So Bwgan the scarecrow scrambled down the

hill with Cleo and Mr Kidwelly. He waited until they were safely back in the house. Then he scrambled back up to the top of the ridge.

Cleo stood on the stool, to bolt the back door. Then she waited for Mr Kidwelly to curl up in his warm basket and go to sleep, so she could turn off the electric light.

Before she climbed into her own bed, Cleo went to the window. She opened it and searched the forest until she saw the scarecrow dancing under the moon. She waved to him and he waved back.

At last, Cleo got into bed and pulled the duvet around her.

'I must remember to knit him a woolly hat tomorrow,' she said, as she closed her eyes.

Mr and Mrs Skeeter Tidy Up

Every Tuesday evening, the residents of Abergelli Street take out their rubbish bags, ready for the next morning's collection. Mrs Rhossili's bag is full of vegetable peel, left-overs and old magazines. Caradog's bag is filled with biscuit wrappers and colouring books. Cleo's mother fills her bag with all the slippers and gloves that Mr Kidwelly has chewed to pieces. The street is dotted with bulging black bags.

Bwgan, the scarecrow, wraps his long coat around his body and listens to the night wind's icy voice. Below him, the lights in the houses go out one by one. Cleo waves to him from her window before she goes to bed. The street lamps blink at him like stars. He listens to the sounds of the night: the owl's bitter shriek as it searches for prey, the whisper of snow in the air.

A voice from the forest calls softly, 'Is everyone asleep, scarecrow?' The voice sounds like iced velvet. It is Mr Skeeter's voice.

'Everyone is asleep,' says Bwgan. 'It's so cold tonight, even the badgers are dreaming long winter dreams, like the squirrels. It is safe to come out now, Mr Skeeter.'

Mr Skeeter is silent as snow. He stretches his long body on the ice-capped earth. He raises his long head and sniffs the air. Mrs Skeeter covers her cubs with blankets of tree-bark. She eases her body out of the lair and hides the entrance under a layer of leaves and tree-bark.

'Good evening, scarecrow,' says Mrs Skeeter.

'Good evening, Mr and Mrs Skeeter,' says Bwgan. 'And how are your cubs tonight?'

'Busy, as usual,' says Mrs Skeeter. 'I've tucked them up and told them to go to sleep. Will you keep an eye on them for me? They don't know the dangers of a frozen night.'

'I'll watch out for them with pleasure. Where are you off to tonight?'

'To Abergelli Street,' says Mrs Skeeter. 'It's Tuesday, isn't it?

'Has Tuesday come round again so soon?' asks Bwgan. 'Well, I never. You'll be busy, then.'

The Skeeters move down the forest together like two stealthy shadows. When they come to a frozen pool, they slide across its glassy surface onto the edge of the forest. Frosted leaves crackle under their feet.

At last, Mr and Mrs Skeeter stand on the sparkling pavement of Abergelli Street. They explore the silence, checking that no one is about.

Their velvet feet make no sound in the darkness. Mrs Skeeter stops to look in the window of Siop y Gornel and marvels at the objects displayed there. 'Humans are very strange,' she says, staring at the display boxes and wondering what they are. She catches sight of her reflection in the shop window and moves her head from side to side, admiring herself.

'You really are a good-looking fox,' agrees Mr Skeeter, as he tackles the black bag on the step of Siop y Gornel. Gently, he eases the black knot between his sharp teeth and opens the bag with his long claws.

Mrs Skeeter helps him spread the contents on the pavement, careful to make no sound. She pulls out envelopes and paper, rolls of cardboard and some out-of-date bars of chocolate. 'Just the thing for the children,' says Mrs Skeeter. 'They can play with the paper and eat the chocolate.' She returns the rubbish to the bag carefully and helps Mr Skeeter tie a knot, using her sharp claws.

They lift up the black bag in their teeth, careful not to tear it, and make their way slowly up Abergelli Street. They carry it up to the forest, watching out for rough stones. They slide the bag across the glassy surface of the pool. Then up, up they carry it until they reach their lair.

'The children are asleep,' says Mrs Skeeter, looking in at the mouth of the den. Her cubs are curled into furry round balls. Their bodies move gently as they dream of scampering among the trees. 'Three beautiful children,' says Mrs Skeeter, proudly.

Down they go again to Abergelli Street. Their velvet paws take them to Cleo's house. Mrs Skeeter looks in through the kitchen window, and watches Mr Kidwelly growling in his dreams. She sees his warm bed with its fleecy lining and his dish of best dog food. She wonders what it

would be like to be looked after, to live in a warm house and have a human to provide food. For a long moment, she wishes her family had all the things that Mr Kidwelly has. Then she sees the collar and lead hanging on the back door and she remembers how lucky she is to be free.

Mr and Mrs Skeeter work through the night, lifting the black bags and carrying them to their lair. They tiptoe over Councillor Pizza's vegetable garden and fetch his rubbish bag from his back door. When they open the bag, they see a pile of Autumn leaves and some empty soup tins. 'This is no use to us,' they say. They tie the bag up and leave it on the pavement. Then they go to look for more bags. They have no time to look up at the stars or listen to the sounds of the night. They have to take all the bags up to their den before the humans wake.

At last, when dawn begins to light up the sky, they stop outside Mr Rhossili's house. Even though they are very quiet, they wake up the pigeons. The pigeons see the Skeeters open up Mrs Rhossili's black bag.

'Wake up, Mr Silly,' cry the pigeons. 'The burglars are here.'

But Mr Rhossili is dreaming of riding the sky in a helicopter and he does not hear their cries.

'Wake up, Mrs Rhossili,' shout the pigeons. 'The burglars are taking your rubbish bag.'

'It's not burglars,' says Mrs Rhossili in her sleep, 'it's the dustmen.' She dreams of sailing downriver on a hippopotamus. Jungle dreams.

The pigeons fly down to question the Skeeters. 'Are you the dustmen?' they ask.

'No, we are not,' says Mr Skeeter, dragging a half-eaten meat pie from Mrs Rhossili's black bag and taking a bite from it.

'Leave that pie alone,' say the pigeons. 'That

bag and all the rubbish belongs to Mrs Rhossili and us pigeons.'

Mr Skeeter opens his wide mouth and snarls at the pigeons. His long teeth flash in the early light, eyes shining silver. Mrs Skeeter joins him. She growls at the pigeons and stretches her sharp claws in their direction. The pigeons fly up to the safety of their nest. They mutter nervously to each other. 'Did you see those horrid eyes? Those foxes can turn quite nasty, can't they? Let them take the black bags . . . we don't care. We'd better stay up here where it's safe.'

Mrs Skeeter finds an old blanket in Mrs Rhossili's bag. 'Just the thing for the cubs,' she says. 'Snow and ice are on the way.'

They carry the last rubbish bag to the end of the road, just in time. The milkman's van is just turning the corner into Abergelli Street. It clatters up to Pedr Pizza's house and Morley the Milk delivers a pint of his best breakfast milk.

The Skeeters carry the last bag up to their lair. Then, as light spreads over the forest, they sort out the rubbish. The food and toys go into the den, the old blanket goes over the cubs, and Mrs Skeeter spreads the newspapers over the entrance, to keep out the snow-laden wind. Mr Skeeter digs a large hole in the ice-bound earth. It's hard work, but it must be done. Then he fills the hole with all the unwanted rubbish. He covers the rubbish with earth, scrabbling away with his paws. He brushes autumn leaves over the top of the earth, using his bushy tail.

'It's daytime,' says Mrs Skeeter. 'Time for bed.'

Mr Skeeter yawns and curls up with Mrs Skeeter and the cubs.

Down below, in Abergelli Street, Mrs Rhossili wakes up and looks out of the window. 'Oh good,' she says, 'the dustmen have been. They've taken everyone's rubbish bags except Councillor Pedr Pizza's. I wonder why.'

Councillor Pedr Pizza
and Uncle Helogan

Winter came early to Abergelli Street. The wind howled at the doors and threw snowflakes at the windows. The pigeons turned their nest upside down and hid under it for protection and Cleo knitted the scarecrow a long floppy scarf to keep him warm up in the forest.

Councillor Pedr Pizza loved summer and hated winter. He missed the bright yellow summer sun and hated having cold toes. Every winter morning, he went to the front door to get his bottle of milk. Every winter morning, he boiled the milk in a saucepan and made himself a hot cup of breakfast cocoa. Then he put on his woolly gloves and went out to water the ruby red geraniums in his greenhouse.

One day, when snow covered the doorstep and Councillor Pizza's toes were colder than ever, he went to get his bottle of milk. It was gone. There was just a deep round hole in the snow where the bottle had been standing.

'Someone's taken my milk,' exclaimed Councillor Pedr Pizza.

He looked down and saw footsteps leading away from the front door. There were dark little triangles everywhere. 'Those triangles are from the pigeons' feet,' said Councillor Pizza. 'But the pigeons can't have taken my milk. The bottle is too slippery for their feet to hold.'

Councillor Pedr Pizza saw other footsteps leading away from the door. There were clusters of dots everywhere. 'I know those footsteps,' said Councillor Pizza. 'They belong to the marmalade cat from Siop y Gornel. But she likes cream, not milk. She hasn't taken my milk bottle.'

Then he saw a wonky line of very strange footprints. They looked like splayed fingers, but long and narrow and very deep. The wonky line went past the front door and round beyond the back door. Councillor Pizza put on his snow boots and followed the wonky line round to the back garden.

Councillor Pedr Pizza saw that snow had covered his fruit bushes and vegetables with a thick white blanket. Then he looked at the wonky line . . . it led straight to the greenhouse. He opened the door and saw a small blue dragon sitting in a corner among the geraniums, shivering.

'What are you doing in my greenhouse?' asked Councillor Pizza.

'Shivering,' said the dragon.

'You haven't seen a milk-bottle, have you?' asked Councillor Pizza.

'I might have,' said the dragon. His teeth were chattering so much, Councillor Pedr Pizza could hardly make out what he was saying.

'Did you take my milk bottle from the front door?'

The dragon nodded. 'I might have.'

'Well, what have you done with it? I need it for my cocoa.'

'I ate it for breakfast,' said the dragon.

'Well, I never,' said Councillor Pizza, 'I didn't know dragons ate milk bottles.'

'Only if we're very hungry,' said the dragon. 'And I am still hungry. Would you like to invite me in to sit by your nice warm fire? I'm really very cold, too.'

Councillor Pizza looked at the blue dragon shivering in the corner of the greenhouse. 'Are you dangerous?' asked Councillor Pizza. 'I've never met a dragon before. Is it safe to let you into my house?'

'Of course it's safe,' said the blue dragon. 'My name is Uncle Helogan. I live in a cave at the top of the forest, but it's full of white stuff now.' His teeth chattered so much, they played a tune.

'My feet are aching,' he said. 'It's such a long walk down the forest.'

'You walked?' said Councillor Pizza, looking at Uncle Helogan's wings. 'I thought dragons could fly.'

'It's far too cold for my wings to work,' said the dragon, sneezing.

'You need warming up,' said Councillor Pizza. 'I suppose you'd better come in for a nice cup of black tea. Come on. Follow me.'

Uncle Helogan followed Councillor Pizza into the house. He watched the councillor fill the kettle and put it on the ring to boil. Then Uncle Helogan settled himself down in the front room, right by the fire. As he warmed up, his colour gradually changed from blue to bright green and his tail grew longer and longer.

'Well, that is interesting,' said Councillor Pizza. 'I didn't know that dragons could change colour. Do you take sugar?'

'Take sugar? Where to?'

'I mean do you take sugar in your tea?' asked Councillor Pizza, pouring hot water onto tea-bags.

Uncle Helogan did not answer. He didn't know what sugar was. So Councillor Pizza put three spoonfuls of sugar in his tea and stirred it, then he handed the cup and saucer to Uncle Helogan.

Uncle Helogan was a lovely shade of orange by now. *'Diolch.* Thank you for the tea,' he said politely. He put the cup and saucer into his mouth and swallowed them both.

'Goodness me,' said Councillor Pizza, 'Do dragons eat crockery?'

'That was very tasty,' said Uncle Helogan. 'Do you have any more?'

'That was my best cup and saucer,' said Councillor Pizza.

But Uncle Helogan did not hear him. He was too busy eating Councillor Pizza's newspaper.

'Stop that,' said Mr Pizza. 'I haven't read it yet.'

Uncle Helogan did not hear him. He was too busy eating Councillor Pizza's spectacles.

'Stop that! ' shouted Councillor Pizza. 'I've got nothing to read and nothing to read it with now.'

Uncle Helogan looked up. 'Are you shouting at me?'

'Yes, I am,' said Councillor Pizza. 'You are eating all my things, You aren't supposed to eat newspapers and spectacles.'

'I'm sorry,' said Uncle Helogan. He was now twice as big and his colour had changed again. He was bright red, with orange ears. 'I haven't been inside a house before. Am I allowed to eat that wooden thing?'

'No, you are not,' said Councillor Pizza. 'That is my Mam-gu's Eisteddfod chair. It's been in my family a long time and it wants to go on being in my family. If you intend staying here, you mustn't eat the chairs or the table or the carpets or the curtains. You can't eat the cups or the plates or the television or my guitar. And you mustn't eat my beautiful flowers or my prize leeks.'

'Oh dear,' said the dragon. 'But I'm still hungry. What can I eat?'

'How about a tin of soup?' asked Councillor Pizza. He showed the dragon a tin of tomato soup.

'That will be fine, thank you,' said the Uncle Helogan. He picked up the tin of soup and swallowed it.

'Oh, well,' said Councillor Pizza. 'It saves using the tin-opener, I suppose. And there'll be no washing-up to do.'

'I like it here,' said Uncle Helogan, 'it's warm and friendly. I like the hot fire and the tin of soup. I like you, Councillor Pizza. May I stay with you until the cold white stuff's gone away?'

'You've grown too big for my house now,' said Councillor Pizza.

'No problem,' said the dragon. He snorted twice and waved his tail about until he became a small golden dragon. 'Now can I stay?'

Councillor Pizza looked hard at Uncle Helogan. He was a beautiful golden colour now. Golden light streamed out of his scales, as if the golden summer sun had come to stay in Councillor Pizza's living-room.

'Alright,' said Councillor Pizza, 'you can stay, so long as you don't eat any more of my furniture.'

'Thank you,' said Uncle Helogan. And he curled up into a bright yellow ball in front of the fire and went to sleep.

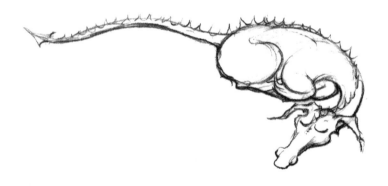

Brinley Baseball Goes Flying

Spring came at last to Abergelli Street, There were buds in the trees and flowers in the gardens. Councillor Pizza transplanted his prize vegetables, the pigeons turned their nest the right way up and Brinley Baseball left his buttercup field to go for an invigorating walk.

Brinley never looked where he was going. He was always walking into things. On Monday, he walked into a lamp-post, on Tuesday he walked into the library by mistake and on Wednesday he walked into Mrs Rhossili and her shopping. Tins of pigeon food and packets of chocolate sauce (Caradog's favourite) rolled all over the pavement.

'Sorry,' said Brinley. He helped Mrs Rhossili pick up all the tins and packets and then he helped her carry them home.

'You really should look where you're going,' said Mrs Rhossili, as they walked up the steps to her front door.

'I love watching clouds,' said Brinley. 'Have you seen the way they change shapes as they float around the sky?'

'It's all very well to gaze at clouds,' said Mrs

Rhossili, getting her key from her coat pocket, 'but you're always bumping into things.'

'I know,' said Brinley, 'but there's so much to watch in the sky. Have you seen all the birds swimming up there? I wish I had wings.'

'Donkeys don't have wings,' said the pigeons, laughing. 'They have big ears and clompy feet. We don't want a donkey in our flying space.'

When Brinley left Mrs Rhossili's house, he went to visit Councillor Pizza and Uncle Helogan. They were weeding the vegetable garden.

'Does anyone want to come for a walk?' he asked.

'No thanks,' said Uncle Helogan. 'I'll be doing some flying later on. My wings are working now that the weather's perked up.'

'I wish I could fly,' said Brinley, mournfully. He saw a kite high up in the sky. He was so busy watching it swaying in the high winds, he didn't notice Cleo and Mr Kidwelly coming towards him. His feet got entangled in Mr Kidwelly's lead.

'Watch where you're going,' said Cleo, kneeling to unwind the lead.

'Sorry,' said Brinley. 'I was watching that kite. Just look at the way it dances in the sky. I wish I was a kite.'

'I'm glad you're not a kite,' said Cleo. 'You'd look rather silly, floating up there with your long tail and your four flinty hooves.'

But Brinley wanted to float high above Abergelli Street, like Uncle Helogan and the pigeons. He made up his mind there and then to do something about it. He strutted down Abergelli Street, head held high and tail swishing proudly.

Caradog looked out of the window. 'Good morning, Brinley.'

'Coming for a walk, Caradog? This is the day I'm going to fly.'

'I have to tidy my bedroom,' said Caradog. 'Ask me tomorrow and I'll be glad to join you.'

'How about you, pigeons?' asked Brinley, looking up at the roof. 'Are you coming to watch me fly?'

'We're spring-cleaning our nest,' said Deri, Dai, Dylan, Digri and Twp. 'Ask us tomorrow and we'll still say NO. You're making a fool of yourself, Brinley Baseball. Donkeys can't fly.'

There were pigeon feathers all over the road. Brinley collected them into a bag. Then he trotted up the stony lane to the forest. The scarecrow was asleep among the feathery trees. Brinley put his bag down and started to collect fir-tree branches. He put those in his bag, too. Then he started off again up the stony path. This time, the sound of his hooves ringing on the stones woke the scarecrow.

'Good morning, Brinley,' said Bwgan, yawning.

'Sorry to wake you,' said Brinley.

'I'm glad you did,' said Bwgan. 'I'm on guard duty. What have you got in your bag?'

'Oh, just some feathers and flying branches,' said Brinley. 'They're going to help me fly. I'm going to climb to the top of the mountain and use the feathers and leaves to help me. Would you like to come with me and watch me fly?'

'I'll come a little way with you,' said the scarecrow. 'But I can't go far when I'm on duty.'

Bwgan and Brinley went up the forest, weaving in and out of the green slopes. 'This is as far as I go,' said the scarecrow, after a while. He stopped and looked out across the wide bands of pointy green leaves, 'I feel like a cloud myself,' he said. 'We are so high up. Are you sure you're going on?'

'Quite sure,' said Brinley.

'Well, be careful.'

'I will,' said Brinley. 'I'll see you again on the way down. Watch out for a flying donkey.'

Brinley was tired, but he didn't stop. He climbed higher and higher until he reached a small cave on the brow of the mountain. There were strange noises coming from inside the cave.

'Anyone in there?' shouted Brinley, nervously. He poked his head into the cave. It was very dark and his voice echoed from wall to wall.

'*Dewch i mewn*,' shouted a gruff voice. 'Come on in.'

Brinley was scared. Who was shouting in that deep, hollow voice?

'I'm not coming in,' he said. 'You come out and show yourself. I want to see what you look like.' He was very worried now. Who was living in the cave? Perhaps it was a dinosaur with big curvy teeth or a monster pigeon. He listened to the footsteps coming towards him and he shivered.

Brinley was most surprised to see Mr Rhossili coming out of the cave.

'What are you doing up here, Mr Rhossili?'

'This is Uncle Helogan's cave,' said Mr Rhossili. 'He said I could use it for a while, because he's so comfortable at Councillor Pizza's. I've been making myself a secret present. Wait there and I'll show you.'

Mr Rhossili dragged a large object out of the cave. It had paper wings and a seat big enough for two. 'This is my glide-plane,' he said. 'It glides a bit and it's got a propellor. I am going to fly in the sky, far away from those pigeons.'

'Please take me with you,' said Brinley. 'I want to fly, too. I've brought a bag of feathers to help. We can fix them to your glide-plane, if you like.'

'Alright,' said Mr Rhossili, 'I'd be happy to take you.'

While Brinley fixed the feathers onto the tail of the glide-plane, Mr Rhossili turned the propellor. It whirred and whirred. 'We're ready,' said Mr Rhossili, at last. 'Hop in.' Brinley jumped onto the seat. The glide-plane wobbled a bit, then settled down.

They were off. Below them, roads were silvery rivers and around them, clouds glistened in the sunlight. The glide-plane drifted in the air currents and cast pale shadows over the green slopes of the forest.

Bwgan looked up and waved at Brinley as the glide-plane hovered on the tip of the pointy trees. Then it sailed into the air again, towards Abergelli Street. They floated over Councillor Pizza's garden and over Cleo's house, then hovered above Mr Rhossili's roof. Mrs Rhossili was sitting in the garden, reading a newspaper. She looked up and waved to them. Brinley and Mr Rhossili waved back.

'Make sure you're home in time for tea,' said Mrs Rhossili, as they floated over the garden.

Dai, Deri, Dylan, Digri and Twp looked up from their spring-cleaning. 'Look at that Brinley,' they said. 'He's floating in our sky.'

'No, I'm not,' said Brinley, happily. 'I'm flying, really flying at last!'

Midsummer Magic

Once a year, on Midsummer's Day, Bela Gwrach pays a visit to Abergelli Street. Early in the morning, before the sun is up, she combs her orange hair and puts on her best dress. Then she sets off down the road, carrying her big black case. It's a long walk and the case is heavy, but she sings softly to keep herself company.

Mr Kidwelly can hear her coming. He runs to the window, long ears pricked up for sound. Bela's songs remind him of his mother's warm voice; he can hear again the soft whimperings of his brothers and sisters in their basket. He starts to whimper too, remembering his puppy time. But then the sound changes: now he hears Cleo's laughter as she throws him a ball. He wags his tail and barks happily.

'What is it, Mr Kidwelly? Why all the fuss?' asks Cleo, yawning. She gets out of bed and joins him at the window. She sees the rising sun sweeping the shadows off the hills and polishing the slate roofs. Then she sees Bela Gwrach walking past Brinley's buttercup field. Cleo opens the window and hears the music of . . . waterfalls rippling down the mountainside, wild breezes stirring high trees and the sharp cry of a hawk wheeling round in the sky, wheeling, wheeling. She waves to Bela and runs downstairs to search for her recorder.

Brinley Baseball, the donkey, was sleeping when Bela Gwrach came past. He wakes to echoes of her voice. Her song reminds him of his colt days, racing round and round his field. Her song tells of the glory times riding Mr Rhossili's glider. He brays loudly to the sky. Then he looks up the road to see Bela walking off towards Abergelli Street carrying her heavy case. 'Wait for me, Bela,' he calls.

Caradog is writing postcards home, telling his cat cousins about his holiday in Abergelli Street. He writes of chocolate cake and pigeons. He is just starting to tell them about Mr and Mrs Rhossili when he hears Bela coming. Her song is the rhythm of the Abergelli train and her voice is a marmalade cat purring in a tall tree. He goes to the window and watches Bela carrying her black case, shaped like a figure eight. Just behind Bela trots Brinley Baseball. Caradog puts down his postcards and goes to look for his drum kit.

Mrs Rhossili is pruning the roses when she

hears Bela's voice floating past. She remembers all her dreams . . . they float in front of her eyes. Dreams of mountain pools and jungle cries. Dreams of the days she walked everywhere hand in hand with Mr Rhossili. '*Bendigedig!*' she says, excitedly. 'Bela Gwrach is on the way.' She runs up to her bedroom to find a comb.

Uncle Helogan has been out for an early morning flying trip, dragon-style. On his way back, he looks down and sees Bela and Brinley sitting on the stone step outside Siop y Cornel. He glides down and lands at Bela's feet.

'Hello,' says Bela, 'Who are you? I haven't seen you before.'

'Uncle Helogan at your service. Want a bonfire started? If so, I'm your dragon. I'm staying with Councillor Pedr Pizza,' he says. 'Have you come to stay here, too?'

'No,' says Bela 'I've just come for the Midsummer's Day jam session.'

'Jam?' says Uncle Helogan. 'Oh, dear. There is no jam. I've eaten every jar of jam in Siop y Gornel. There's no strawberry jam and no apricot jam and no gooseberry jam . . . not even a jar of pickle.'

'I don't mean that sort of jam,' says Bela. She

opens the big black case and brings out her cello. 'A jam session means making music together. Just you watch.'

Mrs Rhossili arrives with a breakfast tray for Bela. There are two brown boiled eggs, some toast fingers and a large mug of tea. 'Rhossili will be here any minute,' she says. 'He's searching for his trumpet. And the pigeons are bringing along some spoons.'

As soon as Bela's eaten her breakfast, she opens the figure eight case and brings out her cello. She picks up her bow and starts to play. A river of music pours out of the cello and coloured sparks shoot out of her bow.

Mrs Rhossili puts a piece of paper over the comb and starts to play some tingly music. Then the pigeons arrive, carrying spoons in their mouths. They all have teaspoons except Twp: he's carrying a ladle. They fly above Bela's head, banging the spoons together. The music rises above the rooftops and glistens in the sun.

Here comes Mr Rhossili, marching down the street. He plays a mean trumpet.

Cleo arrives with her recorder. She can only play one tune, but she plays it slow, then fast, then upside down and backwards. Mr Kidwelly barks every time she takes a breath.

The music gathers pace. Bela disappears inside the cello as it twirls round and round in a cloud of pink smoke, throwing music out everywhere.

Councillor Pedr Pizza and Caradog arrive with their drums. Councillor Pizza plays strict time, military style. Caradog just bangs when the mood takes him. Brinley's hooves sound like a steel band.

Music has come to Abergelli Street. Windows quiver in its presence as Bela's jazzy sounds

bounce from door to door. It floats up into the air,
over the houses and the stony mountain path, to
where Bwgan, the scarecrow, keeps guard. It tickles
his flat ears and sets his feet tapping. It reminds
him of his dancing days when he jumped about
with Gwilym's black lambs. He dances down the
mountainside on a moving belt of music.

When evening shadows lap at the sky, Mr and
Mrs Skeeter wake their sleeping cubs. 'Listen,'
they say, 'Bela's brought music.'

The cubs follow Mr and Mrs Skeeter down the mountainside, tumbling and rolling in the music. When they reach Abergelli Street, they hide among the evening shadows, watching the music grow richer and richer.

They see the pigeons clashing their shrill spoons, they hear drums throbbing. Bwgan's low voice is singing his dreams and Uncle Helogan is blowing 'Oom-Pa-Pa' smoke rings. The cubs stay in the shadows, tails wagging in time to the music.

Bela is stirring the music with her long bow. She gazes into the shadows and smiles. Then she plays for the Skeeters. She plays the music of forest and stream, the whisper of leaves in the nestling trees, the scamper of squirrels in the undergrowth, the lone wolf howling at the moon. Mr and Mrs Skeeter raise their heads and howl to Bela's music. Even the cubs join in, squeaking off key.

When the moon opens the golden clouds, Bela stops playing. One by one, the others stop playing, too. Mrs Rhossili says, 'Lovely music. *Diolch*, Bela.' She tucks her arm in Mr Rhossili's and they go home, followed by pigeons dropping spoons. 'Just leave the spoons where they fall,' says Dai. 'Caradog will pick them up for us later.'

But Caradog has fallen asleep on the stone step

of Siop y Gornel, next to Uncle Helogan and Brinley. They snore in harmony.

Cleo gives Bela a hug. 'See you next year, Bela. I'll have my piccolo by then.' Mr Kidwelly wags his tail, barks and follows Cleo home.

'That was a good jam session,' said Bwgan, as he helps Bela pack away her cello.

Bela yawns, 'I think I'll take a little nap in Uncle Helogan's cave,' she says. 'I've another busy day tomorrow.'

Bela, Bwgan and the Skeeters climb up the forest under the stars. The cubs are complaining, 'Our legs are tired. Carry us.' They climb onto their father's back and go to sleep.

Green shadows meet them as they enter the forest. The shadows hide them from sight.

Good night, Abergelli Street. See you in the morning.

I wrote my first story when I was five and I've been writing ever since. I loved working on this book of stories with Elaine the illustrator. I also love gardening, cats, walking by water and playing the piano. My daughters Sian and Bela are musicians; the cellist on the cover looks a little like Bela, except she doesn't wear a witch's hat.

Look out for my poetry book . . . it's called *Star in the Custard*.

Nicola

Here are some Welsh words used by characters in the stories – and their meanings:

Bendigedig	–	Wonderful
Dere 'mlaen	–	Come on
Dewch i mewn	–	Come in
Diolch	–	Thank you
Siop y Gornel	–	the Corner Shop